Title: Tony Stewart
R.L.: 1.7
PTS: 0.5
TST: 110371

NASCAR Champions

TONY STEWART

Greg Roza

PowerKiDS press™

New York

Published in 2007 by The Rosen Publishing Group, Inc.
29 East 21st Street, New York, NY 10010

Book Design: Michael J. Flynn

Photo Credits: Cover (Stewart) © Ezra Shaw/Getty Images; cover (background) © Chris Stanford/Getty Images; pp. 5, 13, 21 © Rusty Jarrett/Getty Images; pp. 7, 9 © David Taylor/Allsport; p. 11 © Jamie Squire/Getty Images; p. 15 © Jonathan Ferrey/Getty Images; p. 17 © Robert Laberge/Getty Images; p. 19 © Streeter Lecka/Getty Images.

Library of Congress Cataloging-in-Publication Data

Roza, Greg.
  Tony Stewart / Greg Roza.
      p. cm. — (NASCAR champions)
  Includes index.
  ISBN-13: 978-1-4042-3456-X
  ISBN-10: 1-4042-3456-X (lib. bdg.)
  1. Stewart, Tony, 1971—Juvenile literature. 2. Stock car drivers—United States—Biography—Juvenile literature. I. Title. II. Series.
  GV1032.S743R69 2007
  796.72092—dc22
  (B)
                    2006014307

Manufactured in the United States of America

"NASCAR" is a registered trademark of the National Association for Stock Car Auto Racing, Inc.

Contents

Tony Stewart is a race car driver. He started racing go-karts when he was 7 years old.

5

Tony began racing Indy cars in 1996. Indy cars are low cars with uncovered wheels.

7

Tony won an Indy car championship in 1997.

9

Tony also likes to race
pickup trucks.

10

11

Tony started racing stock cars in 1998. Stock cars look like the cars people drive on roads.

13

Tony was named NASCAR Rookie of the Year in 1999. That year, he drove in two races in a single day!

Tony won his first NASCAR championship in 2002. He won three races that year.

Tony won his second NASCAR championship in 2005. He won five races that year.

18

Tony likes to help people. He helps raise money for sick children.

21

Glossary

championship (CHAM-pea-uhn-ship) A contest held to see who is the best in a sport.

go-kart (GOH–kahrt) A small car that is sometimes used in races.

pickup truck (PIHK-uhp TRUHK) A small truck that usually has an open bed in the back.

rookie (RU-kee) Someone who is in their first year in a sport.

Books and Web Sites

Books

Leebrick, Kristal. *Tony Stewart*. Mankato, MN: Capstone Press, 2004.

Teitelbaum, Michael. *Tony Stewart: Instant Superstar!* Chanhassen, MN: Child's World, 2002.

Web Sites

Due to the changing nature of Internet links, PowerKids Press has developed an online list of Web sites related to the subject of this book. This site is updated regularly. Please use this link to access the list:
http://www.powerkidslinks.com/NASCAR/stewart/

23

Index